THE MOVIE STORYBOOK

EGMONT

We bring stories to life

First published in Great Britain 2011 by Egmont UK Limited
239 Kensington High Street, London W8 6SA

Thomas the Tank Engine & Friends™

CREATED BY BRITT ALLCROFT

Based on the Railway Series by the Reverend W Awdry
© 2011 Gullane (Thomas) LLC. A HIT Entertainment company.
Thomas the Tank Engine & Friends and Thomas & Friends are
trademarks of Gullane (Thomas) Limited.
Thomas the Tank Engine & Friends and Design is
Reg. U.S. Pat. & Tm. Off.

HiT entertainment

ISBN 978 1 4052 6005 3
49981/1
Printed in Italy

One day, on the Island of Sodor, Thomas was puffing along the main line when he saw a scary sight. Dark grey smoke and bright orange flames were coming out of an old farm shed!

"Fire!" Thomas peeped in alarm.

"Over here, Thomas!" called his best friend, Percy, who was helping to fight the fire. "We need more water!"

So Thomas pulled up and let the Firemen take bucketfuls of water out of his boiler to throw on the flames.

But the fire would not go out. Thomas and Percy **wheeshed** with worry.

The Fat Controller was worried, too. "We must not let the fire spread," he told the engines. "Sodor will be in **danger!**"

Suddenly, a big, blue engine named Belle arrived, ringing her brass bell. **Clang-clang!** "I can help!" she said, bravely. With a **rumble** and a **rush**, then a **gurgle** and a **gush**, water shot out of two spouts high on Belle's tanks and onto the flames. Thomas and Percy were very surprised!

With Belle's extra water, the fire was soon put out.

"You are all Really Useful Engines," The Fat Controller smiled. "Thomas, you are to show Belle around Sodor today. Percy, your mail trucks are waiting."

Percy was disappointed as he watched Thomas and Belle **puff** off, talking and laughing.

Later, he ran into them at the Steamworks, but they **chuffed** off together before Percy could even **peep** hello.

At Tidmouth Sheds that night, Percy was eager to talk to Thomas about the fire. But Thomas and Belle were tired from their tour of Sodor and went straight to sleep.

The next day, Percy saw Thomas and Belle at the Docks.

"Belle and I are taking the children to the seaside. Goodbye, Percy!" peeped Thomas.

Diesel slid up on the next track as Percy sadly watched them go. "Your best friend doesn't have time for you any more," Diesel said. "You should find a new friend who does."

Diesels were **devious**, but Percy knew Diesel was right.

"If you came to the Dieselworks, you'd be a very **special** visitor," Diesel remarked as he rolled away. "My friend will have **lots** of time for you!"

Percy felt lonelier than ever. He went to meet Diesel's friend at the Dieselworks. It was a very **old** and **dirty** place. Suddenly, a dark shape slid out of the shadows. It was Diesel 10. **"Welcome, Percy,"** he smiled. "Diesel has been telling me all about you. You're a very special engine. Come in!"

Diesel 10's words raced round and round Percy's rods. Thomas may not think Percy was special, but Diesel 10 did!

With his wheels **wobbling** nervously every inch of the way, Percy followed Diesel 10 into the Dieselworks.

Percy couldn't believe his eyes. The Dieselworks was **grimy**, but it was full of Diesels that he had never seen before!

"Tell us about yourself, Percy," said Diesel 10.

"I pull the mail trucks," he told the Diesels.

"A very **important** job!" Diesel 10 smiled, and that made Percy feel very special. One by one, the Diesels introduced themselves. He met Den, Dart, Salty, Paxton, Norman and Sydney. Now Percy had lots of **new friends!**

"If we're poorly, Den tries to fix us. But our Dieselworks is so old and run-down, we don't even have a crane," said Salty.

Percy frowned. "Did you ask for a new Dieselworks?"

"Yes, but The Fat Controller only cares about Steamies," said Diesel 10, sadly.

An idea flew into Percy's funnel. "I can ask Thomas to tell The Fat Controller. He always listens to Thomas!"

"That's a good idea, Percy. Thank you," Diesel smiled.

Soon after, Percy left the Dieselworks with his **boiler bubbling**. He was happy to help his new friends.

Meanwhile, a new fire engine arrived at the Docks. He and Belle would be part of the new **rescue team** on the Island. The other engines were excited to meet him!

Cranky the Crane lifted him off the boat. "I've never seen an engine like you before," he growled.

"Flynn's the name!" the bright red engine **laughed**.

The Fat Controller asked Thomas to take Flynn around Sodor and introduce him to the other engines.

Later, Percy found Thomas and the other engines at the Steamworks. He wanted to tell them about the Diesels. Everyone would think he was very **special** then!

But before he could peep a word, Percy saw Flynn the fire engine. With his **shiny** red paint and **fancy** fire tools, Flynn looked fast and fearless!

Thomas **whistled**, "The children are waiting to meet you, Flynn." He and Flynn quickly **rushed** off together.

Once again, Percy watched his best friend go. "I'm not **big** and **brave** like Belle, or **fast** and **fearless** like Flynn, but Diesel 10 thinks I'm important," he thought.

Just then, he saw Kevin and remembered what Salty had told him. "Kevin, the Diesels are really friendly!" **peeped** Percy. "But they need a crane. If you went to the Dieselworks, you would be a **hero**."

"**Heaving hooks!** I've never been called a **hero** before. I'll do it!" cried Kevin.

That night, Percy went to ask Thomas to talk to The Fat Controller. He didn't want to let his new friends down. But when he arrived at the Sheds, Percy **screeched** to a stop. Flynn was in Percy's berth, right next to Thomas!

"Hello, Percy. Thomas said I could ease my axles here," said Flynn, brightly.

Percy was very upset! Then he looked at Thomas. He didn't feel like Percy's best friend any more. "You can stay in my place," Percy said to Flynn as he backed away. **"I'm very busy!"**

He decided to help his new friends that night! Taking a flatbed from the Sheds, Percy **raced** to the Steamworks.

"Kevin, I'm taking you to the Dieselworks right now!" said Percy. And before Kevin knew it, he was on the flatbed and being taken inside the Dieselworks.

"Welcome, Kevin!" cried Diesel 10. "You're a real **hero** to us Diesels." Kevin beamed happily as he wheeled off to help Den.

But Diesel 10 was cross that Percy hadn't talked to Thomas yet. "You **must** bring Thomas here. Then he'll have to listen!"

"Yes, I'll bring Thomas," Percy said, his wheels wobbling.

The next morning, Percy chuffed into Knapford Station.

"Percy, where have you been all night?" asked Thomas.

"With my new friends, the Diesels!" Percy puffed, proudly.

"The Diesels!" cried the other engines, their boilers bubbling over in shock.

Just then, Gordon **thundered** into the Station. "Kevin's missing from the Steamworks!" he wheeshed.

Percy smiled. "He's being Really Useful at the Dieselworks."

"Cinders and ashes!" puffed Thomas. "The Diesels have stolen Kevin. We must tell Victor right away!"

At the Steamworks, Percy finally had everyone's attention. "The Dieselworks is old and run-down," he said. "They don't even have a crane! They need Kevin."

Victor was upset. "I need Kevin, too," he said.

Percy looked to Thomas for help, but his best friend was talking to Flynn. That made Percy feel **very cross**. "If you want Kevin back, then Thomas must go to the Dieselworks to fetch him!" he **peeped** loudly.

As Thomas whistled in surprise, Victor steamed, "The Fat Controller must know about this!" and **whooshed** out.

Percy **raced** to the Dieselworks. "Thomas will be here soon, but Victor has gone to tell The Fat Controller," he said.

"Very good, Percy," said Diesel 10, slyly. "Now we can take over the Steamworks, and you will lead us! Then The Fat Controller will listen to us, and you will be our **hero**."

Just then, Thomas arrived, looking for Kevin.

"Hello, Thomas," said Diesel 10. He clashed his claw, tossing sparks around. "Den and Dart will take you to the back shed."

"Help me, Percy!" cried Thomas, as he was shunted away.

"He and I are busy, aren't we?" smiled Diesel 10.

"Yes!" Percy peeped, feeling very grand. And with that, he led the Diesels in a **roaring charge** to the Steamworks!

Arriving at the Steamworks, Percy waited for the Diesels to call him their hero. But they didn't take any notice of him at all.

"Hahaha! The Steamworks is ours! We'll never give it back!" Diesel 10 laughed.

Percy shook with surprise. "You have to give it back after The Fat Controller gives you a new Dieselworks," he peeped.

"No, we don't. Out of my way, you silly Steamie!" cackled Diesel 10, **whizzing** past.

The Diesels went **biffing** into buffers and **twirling** on the turntable. "Silly Steamie! Silly Steamie!" they laughed.

"Bust my buffers," moaned Percy. "Thomas is trapped and the Diesels have stolen the Steamworks. And it's all my fault!"

Percy knew he had to fix his mistakes. "I can't rescue the Steamworks on my own. But I **can** rescue Thomas!"

He steamed to the Dieselworks. But before he could find Thomas, he saw flames inside the main shed. "**Fire!** I must fetch Belle and Flynn!" he cried.

With his **pistons pumping**, Percy sped to the Sodor Search and Rescue Centre to alert them.

Belle clanged her bell as Flynn honked and hooted. "I'm **ready** and **raring** to rescue!" he cried.

"We have no time to lose!" said Percy.

At the Dieselworks, Percy raced straight to the back shed. Den and Dart were blocking Thomas' track to keep him inside.

"Let Thomas go!" urged Percy.

"We have our orders from Diesel 10," said Dart.

"Don't be silly!" barked Percy. "Hurry, the shed is on fire!"

The two Diesels saw the **danger** and fled, leaving the way clear for Thomas. Percy quickly coupled up to Kevin's flatbed and the three friends steamed out of the shed.

"Thank you for rescuing me!" peeped Thomas.

The engines went to the front of the Dieselworks and saw that the **fire** had grown much bigger. The flames **hissed** and **fizzed**, and **flickered** and **flashed**.

Through the **swirling** smoke, they saw Belle and Flynn **fearlessly** fighting the fire.

"Heaving hooks!" said Kevin. "I've never seen a fire before. It's scary."

"Stay back, stay calm. No cause for alarm!" shouted Flynn.

Thomas, Percy and Kevin stayed safely behind the fire engines. They watched as Belle's two spouts and Flynn's long hose soaked the fire with **powerful** jets of water.

Finally, the fire went out. The Dieselworks was **saved!**

"Hooray for Flynn!" cheered Percy.

"Hooray for Belle!" cheered Thomas.

With the fire out, Percy remembered the other danger. "The Diesels have taken over the Steamworks, Thomas!"

"Don't worry, Percy. We'll fetch all our friends. Then we'll **wheesh** and we'll **whoosh** … and we'll win back the Steamworks!" chuffed Thomas.

"Come on, Kevin," Percy cried. "We're taking you home!"

The two friends **raced** along the rails, with Kevin **rolling** and **rattling** on the flatbed. First, they told Edward and Henry. Next, they found Gordon and James. Then, they fetched Emily and Toby.

Together, with steam trailing behind them, the engines flew down the tracks. They were going to save the Steamworks!

Just like he had done with the Diesels, Percy led his steam engine friends to the Steamworks.

Inside, the Diesels were still making a dreadful mess.

"Whoop!" cried Paxton as he heaved on a hoist.

"Whee!" said Diesel 10 as he spun on the turntable.

When the steam engines charged in, the Diesels were very surprised!

"The Steamworks is ours now!" sneered Diesel 10.

"No, the Steamworks is ours. Taking it from us is not right!" Thomas replied.

"You tricked me," Percy told the Diesels. "But we won't trick you. We want to help."

Clank! Diesel 10 snapped his claw loudly. "How will you help us?" he asked, suspiciously.

"We will tell The Fat Controller that the Diesels need a new Dieselworks!" promised Thomas.

Just then, The Fat Controller walked in. "Diesel 10!" he **boomed**. "What do you think you are doing?"

"I … I … erm …" Diesel 10 stammered.

"You have damaged the Dieselworks and the Steamworks! And because of the confusion you have caused, **none** of my engines is being Really Useful," said The Fat Controller, crossly.

Diesel 10 looked at the ground, whimpering.

Percy bravely puffed his **biggest** puff and said, "Sir, Diesel 10 behaved badly because the Dieselworks is **old** and **dirty**."

"It's **grimy** and **greasy**," whistled Thomas.

"They don't even have a crane," added Kevin.

"May the Diesels have a new Dieselworks?" Thomas asked.

The Fat Controller looked at the Diesels, sternly. "Of course, you will have a new Dieselworks. But everyone must wait their turn. You will see that some things are worth waiting for!"

Soon, the rebuilding of the Dieselworks began. And the Steamies and the Diesels all worked together! It was very **rough**, **tough** work, but each day, they all **huffed** and **puffed** their hardest.

Diesel 10, Paxton and Salty shunted trucks here and there, while Den and Dart rattled and rolled along so fast, they became quite **dizzy!**

Thomas and Percy worked side by side. Their fireboxes **fizzed** and their boilers **bubbled** as they laughed together. Henry and Edward **pushed** and **pulled** trucks along the rails. Gordon and Emily whistled as they worked in the Yard. With so much work to do, the Diesels were grateful for the steam engines' help.

At last, the new Dieselworks was finished. It had bright yellow paint and a shiny new sign. All the Diesels gathered in front, feeling very proud of their Dieselworks.

"This is a very special building," said The Fat Controller. "Not because it is new and grand, but because it shows what happens when **Really Useful Engines** work together."

"You are all very **special** and **important engines**. And I am proud of you all," finished The Fat Controller.

"Hear, hear!" said Lady Hatt.

Then the Steamies and the Diesels made a great cheering noise with lots of whistling and honking. Everyone joined in … Even Diesel 10!

Later, puffing back to the Sheds, Percy said, "Thomas?"

"Yes, Percy?"

"When I'm with you, I feel most proud of all, and most special of all," Percy chuffed, happily.

Thomas beamed from **buffer** to **buffer**. "That's exactly how I feel when I'm with you!"

The engines laughed together, as only **best friends** can.